WITHDRAWN

P9-DTP-707

tien
pich

Dear Parents:

Congratulations! Your child is taking the first steps on an exciting journey. The destination? Independent reading!

STEP INTO READING® will help your child get there. The program offers five steps to reading success. Each step includes fun stories and colorful art or photographs. In addition to original fiction and books with favorite characters, there are Step into Reading Non-Fiction Readers, Phonics Readers and Boxed Sets, Sticker Readers, and Comic Readers—a complete literacy program with something to interest every child.

Learning to Read, Step by Step!

Ready to Read   Preschool–Kindergar
• big type and easy words • rhyme and rhythm • ...ure clues
For children who know the alphabet and are eager to begin reading.

Reading with Help   Preschool–Grade 1
• basic vocabulary • short sentences • simple stories
For children who recognize familiar words and sound out new words with help.

Reading on Your Own   Grades 1–3
• engaging characters • easy-to-follow plots • popular topics
For children who are ready to read on their own.

Reading Paragraphs   Grades 2–3
• challenging vocabulary • short paragraphs • exciting stories
For newly independent readers who read simple sentences with confidence.

Ready for Chapters   Grades 2–4
• chapters • longer paragraphs • full-color art
For children who want to take the plunge into chapter books but still like colorful pictures.

STEP INTO READING® is designed to give every child a successful reading experience. The grade levels are only guides; children will progress through the steps at their own speed, developing confidence in their reading.

Remember, a lifetime love of reading starts with a single step!

A special thanks to the wonderful people of the Pacific Islands for inspiring us on this journey as we bring the world of Moana *to life.*

Copyright © 2016 Disney Enterprises, Inc. All rights reserved. Published in the United States by Random House Children's Books, a division of Penguin Random House LLC, 1745 Broadway, New York, NY 10019, and in Canada by Penguin Random House Canada Limited, Toronto, in conjunction with Disney Enterprises, Inc.

Step into Reading, Random House, and the Random House colophon are registered trademarks of Penguin Random House LLC.

Visit us on the Web!
StepIntoReading.com
randomhousekids.com

Educators and librarians, for a variety of teaching tools, visit us at RHTeachersLibrarians.com

ISBN 978-0-7364-3646-5 (trade) — ISBN 978-0-7364-8226-4 (lib. bdg.) —
ISBN 978-0-7364-3647-2 (ebook)

Printed in the United States of America   10 9 8 7 6 5 4 3

Random House Children's Books celebrates the First Amendment and supports the right to read.

Disney

MØANA

Quest for the Heart

by Susan Amerikaner
illustrated by the Disney Storybook Art Team

Random House 🏠 New York

Moana lives on an island.

She loves the island.

Most of all,

she loves the ocean.

The island people do not go

beyond the reef.

This is because

of what happened long ago. . . .

Te Fiti was the mother island.

She gave life to all.

The demigod Maui

used his magic fishhook

to steal her heart.

With no heart,

Te Fiti crumbled.

A terrible darkness spread.
The lava monster Te Kā
struck Maui.
Maui lost his fishhook.
He lost Te Fiti's heart.
Darkness grew.

One day,

the ocean gives Moana

a shiny gift.

It is Te Fiti's heart!

But Moana drops it.

Gramma Tala finds it

and keeps it safe.

Moana grows up.
Her father wants her
to lead her people.
But she is not allowed
to go beyond the reef.

Gramma Tala shows Moana

a secret cave full of old ships.

The island people used to sail
beyond the reef.
They used to be wayfinders!

Gramma Tala gives Moana
the heart of Te Fiti.
She tells Moana to find Maui.
He must return the heart
to Te Fiti.

Moana must sail

beyond the reef.

It is the only way

to save her island.

Moana teaches herself
how to sail.
She sails beyond the reef
into the open ocean.

A storm hits!

The ocean brings Moana

to Maui's island.

Moana meets Maui.

He has many tattoos

that show off his deeds.

Maui thinks he is a hero.

Moana disagrees.

She tells Maui he must return
the heart of Te Fiti.
Maui says no.
He has no power
without his fishhook.

Maui steals Moana's boat.
He sails off without her.
The ocean brings Moana
back to Maui and makes him
teach her to sail.

They must work together
to return Te Fiti's heart.
First, Maui needs to find
his magic fishhook.
Moana will help.

Moana and Maui go
to the world of monsters.
They find a crab monster.
He has Maui's fishhook.
Moana tricks the monster.

She shows him

a shiny stone.

Maui gets his magic fishhook.

His power is back!

He and Moana escape.

Moana and Maui sail to Te Fiti.

Te Kā blocks their way.

Maui uses his fishhook

to change into a huge hawk.

Te Kā strikes Maui

from the sky.

Moana and Maui

do not give up.

Moana sails fast.

She makes Te Kā angry.

She has an idea.

Moana offers the heart of Te Fiti
to Te Kā.

The heart begins to glow.

Te Kā accepts the heart.

Te Fiti returns.

She blooms with plants.

Life returns to all the islands.

Moana and Maui saved the islands!

They saved each other.

They say goodbye.

They will always be friends.

Maui changes back

into a giant hawk.

Moana returns to her island.

Her parents are happy

she is home.

Maui salutes her.

He is Maui,

the hero.

She is Moana,

the great wayfinder.

She is Moana,

the leader of her people!

31901062911328